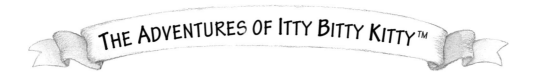

The Adventures of Itty Bitty Kitty™

Library of Congress Cataloging-in-Publication Data

Keeshan, Robert.
Itty Bitty Kitty / by Bob Keeshan ; illustrations by Jane Maday
p.   cm.
Summary: After encountering different animals in the forest and
running for her life, Itty Bitty Kitty finds shelter in a big hotel
with friendly employees.
ISBN 1-57749-017-7
1. Cats—Juvenile fiction. [1. Cats—Fiction. 2. Animals—Fiction.
3. Hotels, motels, etc.—Fiction.] I. Maday, Jane, ill. II. Title.
PZ10.3.K2655It 1997
[E]—dc20   96-27929

First printing: April 1997
Printed in Singapore
00 99 98 97 7 6 5 4 3 2 1

For a current catalog of Fairview Press titles,
please call this toll-free number: 1-800-544-8207

Produced by Mega-Books, Inc.
Design and art direction by Nutshell Design, Inc.

Publisher's Note: Fairview Press publishes books and other materials related to
the subjects of family and social issues. Its publications, including *Itty Bitty Kitty*,
do not necessarily reflect the philosophy of
Fairview Hospital and Healthcare Services or their treatment programs.

Itty Bitty Kitty

by Bob Keeshan

illustrations by Jane Maday

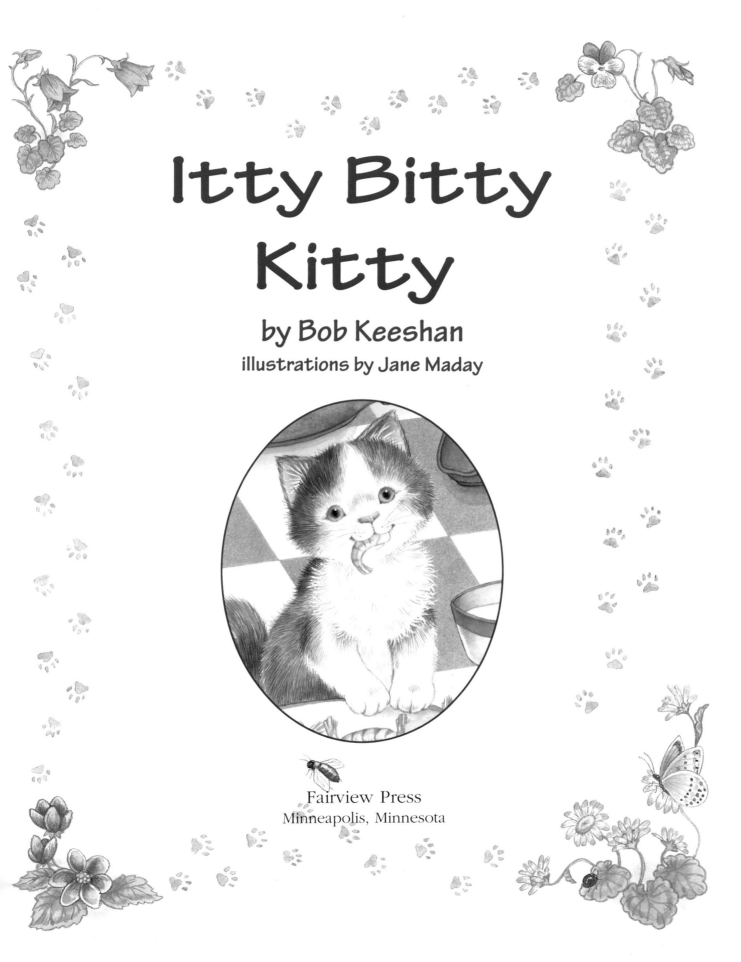

Fairview Press
Minneapolis, Minnesota

One day Itty Bitty Kitty decided to go exploring. She wandered off the porch, around the house, and through the backyard. She was curious about everything she saw — especially the fence at the end of the garden. What could be on the other side?

Itty Bitty Kitty crouched down. She looked at the top of the fence. She wriggled her hips. Suddenly she sprang into the air, but she couldn't jump high enough to get over it.

The tiny kitten sat and scratched behind her ear. There had to be some way to get to the other side. She looked around, and sure enough, there was a small opening in the fence. It was just big enough for Itty Bitty Kitty to squeeze through.

On the other side of the fence, tall trees seemed to touch the sky. A bright orange butterfly caught Itty Bitty Kitty's eye, and she scampered after it. The kitten followed the butterfly farther and farther into the woods. At last it fluttered up into the leaves and disappeared.

Itty Bitty Kitty yawned and stretched. She sharpened her tiny claws on the nearest tree, then turned to go home. It was getting dark, and all she could see were trees all around her. Still, cats are good at finding their way home, and the little kitten started off in the right direction.

Itty Bitty Kitty hadn't gone far when a huge raccoon stepped out from its den in a hollow tree. Small as she was, the kitten arched her back and hissed to warn the raccoon away, but the raccoon snarled and charged straight at her. Itty Bitty Kitty ran.

By the time she had gone far enough to feel safe, clouds covered the sky. A low growl of thunder rumbled through the woods. Itty Bitty Kitty had never heard thunder before. She ducked under a thicket to hide and came face to face with a skunk. It raised its tail and turned its back on her, but the kitten had already fled.

Thunder boomed and lightning flashed through the woods. Now Itty Bitty Kitty didn't know which way to go. Then she saw a hole in the side of a small hill. She ran for it but skidded to a stop when she saw two shining eyes. Out of its den leaped a red fox, hungry for its dinner.

Itty Bitty Kitty ran for her life. She heard the swish of an owl's wings as it swooped down through the trees. The kitten zigzagged through the forest. The owl had missed her, but the fox was still close behind.

Again thunder shook the air. A great bolt of lightning hit a nearby tree. The rain poured down. Itty Bitty Kitty didn't know the fox had stopped chasing her. She was too busy running. All at once a brick wall loomed up in front of her. Sensing that it must lead out of the woods, the frightened kitten followed the wall, looking for somewhere to hide.

At last Itty Bitty Kitty came to a dry place that was brightly lit. There were lots of people coming and going through a door in a large building. The small kitten dodged all the feet and scuttled to the side, where she huddled, trembling.

"Look! It's a kitten," someone said.

"Poor little kitty," said someone else. "She's all wet from the rain."

"If the manager sees her, he'll shoo her away," said a bellhop.

"Mr. Dunhoffer has already gone home for the day," said the doorman. "Let her stay and dry off."

All evening the bellhops carried suitcases around Itty Bitty Kitty and made sure that the hotel guests did not step on her. The small kitten felt safe with the people and dozed under the awning the whole night long. But just in case, she kept one eye open to watch out for the hungry red fox.

Early the next morning, as the sun rose on a clear, cool day, the manager arrived at the hotel. He found all four bellhops lined up in front of the door.

"Good morning, Mr. Dunhoffer," they chanted.

"Good morning," the manager said. *How nice,* he thought. *They've never done that before.*

Hidden by the eight shiny shoes of the bellhops was Itty Bitty Kitty.

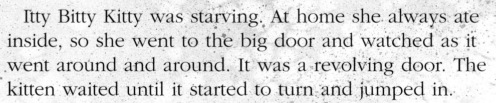

Itty Bitty Kitty was starving. At home she always ate
inside, so she went to the big door and watched as it
went around and around. It was a revolving door. The
kitten waited until it started to turn and jumped in.

Around and around she went, once, twice, three times,
until — *plop!* — Itty Bitty Kitty found herself right back
where she had started.

She tried again and again, and the same thing happened
each time. But the tiny kitten was beginning to understand
how the door worked. On the fourth try, she jumped out
as it opened to the inside.

Itty Bitty Kitty landed in the hotel lobby. Along one side was a long, high counter with desk clerks standing behind it. Itty Bitty Kitty's nose told her she would find what she was looking for on the other side of the lobby. Oh, she was hungry!

Itty Bitty Kitty ran into the dining room. She jumped onto a chair, then up onto the table, knocking over a glass of water. She put her paw on a spoon sticking out of a bowl. It flipped over, spilling sugar into the water.

The kitten was lapping up the delicious sugar water when *swoosh!* she was grabbed from behind and held, oh, so tightly. She growled and hissed and struggled, but she could not get away.

"This must be the kitten the bellhops told us about," said a waitress named Jeannie. "She sure is spunky for such a little thing."

Esmeralda, another waitress, said, "She'll need to be if the manager finds her in here. Let's take her in the kitchen and give her something to eat."

The waitresses gave Itty Bitty Kitty a dish of milk and another of shrimp. The kitten lapped up the milk, keeping an eye on all the feet walking around her. She sniffed at the pieces of shrimp and took a bite. It was very tasty. Itty Bitty Kitty felt *sooo* much better.

Now Itty Bitty Kitty was full, but she was very sleepy. It was too hard to rest with all the people going in and out of the kitchen. She would have to find a place to take a little catnap. Itty Bitty Kitty loved catnaps.

As soon as the kitchen door opened, Itty Bitty Kitty scampered into the dining room.

Breakfast was being served, and the room was filled with people. The kitten made a dash for the lobby. A little boy saw her and tried to catch her, but Itty Bitty Kitty had been too fast for the fox, and she was too fast for the boy. She leaped, caught the bottom of a tablecloth with her claws, and clambered up onto a huge buffet table piled high with food.

"Wow! Look at that!" yelled a little girl.

Itty Bitty Kitty raced down the table. She skidded around the muffins, waded through a mound of scrambled eggs, and sent pieces of bacon flying every which way.

"Cool!" said the little girl's brother.

The kitten jumped off the table. She raced past the cashier's desk and out the door.

Itty Bitty Kitty headed toward the far corner of the lobby, where a fire burned in the fireplace. It was warm and cozy there. Tired and full, the tiny kitten curled up into a ball and fell into a deep, deep sleep.

Justin, one of the bellhops, came over to toss another log on the fire.

"Uh, oh!" he said when he saw Itty Bitty Kitty. "Mr. Dunhoffer had better not see this!"

Just at that very moment, who should appear but the manager.

He looked at the fire and smiled, but his smile faded when he saw the kitten. "Justin! What is that?" he said in his booming voice.

"What is what, sir?" asked Justin.

"That thing in front of my fireplace!" Mr. Dunhoffer bellowed.

Itty Bitty Kitty did not so much as twitch an ear.

"That, Mr. Dunhoffer," said Justin, "is a decoration I thought would look nice. Kind of homelike, having a cat asleep in front of the fire. She looks real, doesn't she?"

"Indeed she does," said Mr. Dunhoffer, leaning over for a closer look. "Looks very real. Great idea, Justin. Keep up the good work."

"Yes, sir!" said Justin with a grin.

Itty Bitty Kitty opened one eye and watched the manager walk away. Then she went back to sleep and dreamed about her new home with its good food, warm fire, nice people — and not a raccoon, a skunk, an owl, or a hungry red fox to worry about. Only Mr. Dunhoffer.